Put Beginning Readers on the Right Track with
ALL ABOARD READING™

The All Aboard Reading series is especially for beginning readers. Written by noted authors and illustrated in full color, these are books that children really and truly *want* to read—books to excite their imagination, tickle their funny bone, expand their interests, and support their feelings. With four different reading levels, All Aboard Reading lets you choose which books are most appropriate for your children and their growing abilities.

Picture Readers—for Ages 3 to 6
Picture Readers have super-simple texts, with many nouns appearing as rebus pictures. At the end of each book are 24 flash cards—on one side is the rebus picture; on the other side is the written-out word.

Level 1—for Preschool through First-Grade Children
Level 1 books have very few lines per page, very large type, easy words, lots of repetition, and pictures with visual "cues" to help children figure out the words on the page.

Level 2—for First-Grade to Third-Grade Children
Level 2 books are printed in slightly smaller type than Level 1 books. The stories are more complex, but there is still lots of repetition in the text, and many pictures. The sentences are quite simple and are broken up into short lines to make reading easier.

Level 3—for Second-Grade through Third-Grade Children
Level 3 books have considerably longer texts, harder words, and more complicated sentences.

All Aboard for happy reading!

To Liam and Conor,
the founders of Snail City—Jane

To Gregg, Lynn & Micaela—R.B.

Library of Congress Cataloging-in-Publication Data is available.

ISBN   0-448-42471-1   (GB)   A   B   C   D   E   F   G   H   I   J
ISBN   0-448-42418-5   (pbk.)   A   B   C   D   E   F   G   H   I   J

ALL
ABOARD
READING™

Level 1
Preschool-Grade 1

Snail
City

By Jane O'Connor
Illustrated by Rick Brown

Grosset & Dunlap • New York

In Snail City
life is slow.
Snails like it that way.
There is no fast food.

There is no fast lane
on the highway.

And it takes years
to get a letter by snail mail.

But the snails don't mind.
They like the slow life.

Well, <u>almost</u> all snails do.

This is a snail named Gail.

She is not like other snails.

Gail started to crawl before
any of the other snail babies.

Her first word was "faster."

Her mom and dad keep
on telling her to slow down.
But she can't.

Gail gets to school
early every day.

She comes in first in every race.

For snails, being first

is the worst.

The last one is the winner.

Today there is a class trip.
Gail is at the head
of the line.

The snail kids are going
to a flower garden.
It is five feet from school.
So it will take a long time
to get there.

Soon Gail is way ahead
of everybody.
"Fast poke!" one kid shouts.

Gail does not care.

The sun feels good.

The wind feels good.

And it feels good to crawl fast.

All at once,
Gail hears something.
"Help! Help!"
Gail crawls around a rock.

Oh, no!

Far away she sees a snail baby.

The snail is going to fall

in the water!

"Hold on!"
Gail shouts.
She crawls
as fast as she can.
But it is no good.
The snail baby
has fallen in the water.
Then Gail sees a twig.
She thinks fast.
She acts fast.

Gail pushes the twig
into the water.
There is a strong wind.
Off she goes!

Gail is going fast—
very, very fast!
She has never gone
this fast before.

Gail saves the snail baby.

"Thank you!" says the snail baby.

"Thank you!"

says the snail mom.

Gail crawls back on her twig.

She goes back
across the water.
The whole snail class
is there.

"We saw what you did!"
says Ms. Slime.
"You are very brave."

No one calls her
a fast poke now.

And everyone sails on a twig.
But they wait until
there is no wind.
That way they can go...
nice and slow!